This book belongs to

....

The King of Spring

Nick and Claire Page

Illustrations by Yannick Robert

make
believe
ideas

The King of Spring was very
bouncy. Everything made
him bounce.

6

When he saw flowers growing or bees buzzing or lambs skipping in the castle meadow, he just had to bounce. And he made everyone else bounce as well.

He made people bounce around town.
He made the Prime Minister bounce while
making VERY IMPORTANT LAWS.

He made the lambs so bouncy that
farmers had to use ladders to get
them out of the trees.

He even put the cows
on trampolines, so the milk came out
all bubbly, like a milkshake.

Only one thing could stop the king bouncing:
the November gremlins, who lived in the castle
attic. They worked for the Winter Wizard, but
they hadn't been seen for years . . .

One day, the King of Spring bounced so high that CRACK! he went straight through the ceiling and into the castle attic. Then WHACK! he hit his head on the roof before falling down again, to land on the Prime Minister!

Now when the king bounced into the attic, something strange had happened. A nasty November gremlin had grabbed him, and was sitting on his shoulder.

"Call yourself a king?" whispered the gremlin. "Kings are sensible and wise, not silly, bouncy fools. You must never, ever bounce again." At that, a small tear rolled down the King of Spring's face.

From then on, the king stopped bouncing.
He just lay on the sofa, staring at the
ceiling. He even wore very heavy boots to
make extra sure he couldn't bounce.

He issued a VERY IMPORTANT LAW, which said: "No one must ever bounce again!" Ball games were banned (except bowls). Balloons were burst. Trampolines were tucked away. And everything bouncy was banned.

Nobody realised that the King of Spring had got a November gremlin. All they knew was that nothing was fun any more. It was not like spring – it was like a very dull, damp, dreary, winter day.

NO BALL GAMES!

FORBIDDEN

NO
SPACEHOPPER

17

One day, the Prime Minister had a
VERY IMPORTANT THINK about all this.
And he remembered how the king had
been bouncy going up into the attic,
and very unbouncy after he came down.

"Aha!" he said, as he looked through
his big book of Winter Wisdom:
"A November gremlin!"

So the Prime Minister crept up to the king while he was having his afternoon nap and pulled his very heavy boots off. "Come on!" he shouted. "We're going for a walk!" And, before he knew it, the king was out of the castle and walking along the streets in his bare feet.

Because he wasn't wearing his heavy
boots, the king felt a bit lighter.
And because everybody seemed so
pleased to see him out and about,
he felt a lot happier.

Then he saw the castle meadow.
He saw flowers growing, and bees
buzzing, and, best of all, lambs skipping
around. They were so happy to see the
king, they bounced extra high and some
of them got caught in the branches.

The King of Spring felt an itch in his feet.
It wriggled up his legs to his knees. Then,
with a great rush, it rippled over him like
a wave and BOING! – the king gave a great
bounce, as high as a tree. (In fact, that was
where he landed, with some of the lambs.)

The November gremlin fell to the ground.
"No!" hissed the gremlin. "Do not bounce!"
SPLAT! The king landed right on the gremlin,
along with seventeen lambs, and squashed
him flat.

After that, the King of Spring bounced everywhere. He had the ceiling in the castle repaired so no one could bounce through it. He brought back the balls and the balloons and all the other bouncy things. And he made a new VERY IMPORTANT LAW: every week the people had to go to the castle meadow and see the lambs. That way, they would be sure to keep on bouncing.

Ready to tell

Oh no! Some of the pictures from this story have been mixed up! Can you retell the story and point to each picture in the correct order?

Picture dictionary

Encourage your child to read these words
from the story and gradually develop his
or her basic vocabulary.

attic

bee

bounce

flowers

gremlin

king

lamb

tree

walk

Key words

Here are some key words used in context. Help your child to use other words from the border in simple sentences.

The king likes to **bounce**.

"No!" says the gremlin.

He is very sad.

He likes to **see** the lambs.

He bounces **up** high.

Spring sports

If it's a sunny day and you feel happy like the King of Spring, why not hold a bouncing competition?

You will need
2 lengths of rope • hoops or beanbags • one ball per contestant • one sack or old pillow case per contestant • a "space hopper" (or two if possible)

What to do
Set out your course, using the ropes to mark the "start" and "finish" lines. Here are some races you could plan:
1 Hop It: a hopping race. You could do this in two laps, hopping first on one leg and then on the other.
2 Bounce Around: a bouncing race. Racers have to jump around beanbags or in and out of hoops that you have put in position, bouncing as high and as far as they can.
3 Bouncing Balls: bouncing a ball as you run the course.
4 Sack Race: bounce to the finish line in large sacks or old pillowcases.
5 The Big Bounce: bounce to the finish line on a "space hopper." If you have only one of these toys, ask a grown-up to time contestants to see who is the quickest.
Can you come up with other fun ideas for your own bouncing races? Good luck and happy bouncing!